Shadow of the Fox

Shadow of the Fox

By Ellen Steiber

BULLSEYE CHILLERS™

RANDOM HOUSE 🏠 NEW YORK

To Sarah Thompson, scholar of old Japan, who actually reads all the books that her friends write and who has so generously shared with me both fox lore and friendship

And with thanks to Bobbi Katz and Cindy Alvarez for being such terrific editors

A BULLSEYE BOOK PUBLISHED BY RANDOM HOUSE, INC.

Text copyright © 1994 by Ellen Steiber
Cover illustration copyright © 1994 by Tim Barrall
All rights reserved under International and Pan-American Copyright Conventions. Published in the United States by Random House, Inc., New York, and simultaneously in Canada by Random House of Canada Limited, Toronto.

Library of Congress Cataloging-in-Publication Data:
Steiber, Ellen.
     Shadow of the fox / by Ellen Steiber.
        p. cm. — (Bullseye chillers)
     SUMMARY: When a mysterious young woman named Mariko saves the life of the samurai Shiro, he falls in love and marries her, only to discover that his wife assumes the shape of a fox at night.
     ISBN 0-679-86667-1 (pbk.)
     [1. Samurai—Fiction. 2. Japan—Fiction. 3. Foxes—Fiction. 4. Horror stories.] I. Title. II. Series.
     PZ7.S81766Sh 1994 [Fic]—dc20 94-1295

Manufactured in the United States of America 10 9 8 7 6 5 4 3 2 1

Contents

Chapter 1

On the Run

The mountains in Japan are very beautiful—and very dangerous. They are filled with hundreds of narrow, winding trails. Bears, wildcats, and foxes roam the forests. Some people say that ghosts and monsters wander across the slopes—and when they rest, they wait for foolish humans.

You can live in the mountains your whole life and still lose your way. There are deep ravines, swift rivers, and sheer cliffs. The mountains are where you go when you want to hide.

I fled to the mountains after betraying my lord. I was a twenty-one-year-old samurai warrior. Like my father and my three older brothers, I lived in Lord Oyama's castle and fought in his army.

But Lord Oyama became cruel when a harsh winter came. When the castle supplies were all gone, he ordered the people in the villages to bring him food. Instead, they streamed into the castle, begging for work. Their farms were buried under snow. There was no food—for us or them.

Lord Oyama sent the villagers back. He demanded that they return with gold. But, of course, they didn't have any. Finally, in early spring, Lord Oyama ordered his samurai to kill the people and raid their homes.

None of the samurai liked these orders. But we were trained to obey without question. Perhaps in my heart I wasn't a true samurai because I couldn't do what my lord asked.

My life with Lord Oyama was over. I had no choice. I left the castle. I told no one of my plan. I took only my sword and knife, my horse, a little food, and some gold coins I'd saved. I knew I'd never see my family again. And I had become a *ronin*, a samurai without a lord. In Japan, that meant I was an outcast.

I headed for the mountains, leaving the castle far behind. I rode the trails until they became too narrow for my horse. Then I led him on foot as we climbed higher. The path wound around like a ribbon pulled from a spool.

When I stopped to let the horse drink from a stream, Lord Oyama's samurai caught up with me. They were disguised as merchants, but I recognized them from the castle. They were older, trusted warriors, two of Oyama's commanders.

"Draw your sword, traitor," ordered the shorter one. "We're here to take your head and carry it back to Lord Oyama."

I drew my sword and fought for my life. It was the hardest battle I had ever fought. They both attacked at once, and they were both master swordsmen. But I was younger and stronger, and I was desperate.

In the end they both lay dead. The sleeve of my robe was stuck to my arm. It was soaked with blood. I'd been badly cut. During the fight, I hadn't even felt the blade go into me. But now my right arm hung limp, and my shoulder felt as if it were on fire.

Darkness was falling, and with it a cold spring rain. I called for my horse. He didn't answer and I soon saw why. The samurai had found him first and slit his throat. He lay in the stream. His blood turned the water red.

My horse was gone. And I was losing strength. I could barely stand upright. I forced myself to keep moving. But soon I could not continue. I collapsed on the dark mountainside, racked with pain, praying that no more soldiers would find me.

The rain continued to fall in a fine, cloudy mist. A strange red moon rose above the trees. And the pain got worse. It was as if the fire in my shoulder flamed through my whole body. I was sure I had a fever. I thought I was going to die.

Then, in the darkness, I saw lights

glowing through the rain. They looked just like torches. Was a family traveling through the mountains? Maybe it was a house. A place where I could get help. With the last of my energy, I crawled toward the lights.

As I got closer to the torches, they seemed to drop to the ground. I covered my head, sure the trees would go up in flame. Instead, an eerie white glow lit the forest floor. I began to shake. Was I delirious? Was this the end? Then darkness swept over me.

Chapter 2

A Strange Warning

Morning light woke me. I was lying inside a small cave. I could hear rain outside, dripping from the trees onto the forest floor.

Fire still burned in my shoulder, but I was no longer bleeding. A thick bandage covered the wound.

"So the samurai finally wakes," said a light voice behind me.

I tried to turn over, but I was still too weak. With a groan, I settled for turning my head. The most beautiful young woman I'd ever seen was sitting beside me. I shut my eyes. Was I dreaming? But when I opened them again she was still there. She had thick black hair that fell to her waist, a small narrow face, and pearl-white teeth. She wore a robe of fine silk. It was orange and gold like autumn leaves. But it was her eyes that amazed me. In Japan most people have dark brown eyes. Her eyes were a tawny gold, the color of topaz.

"You've been sleeping for four days," she said with a laugh.

"What is so funny?" I asked.

"You, samurai," she answered. She tried to look serious but could not hide the laughter in those tawny eyes.

Nothing was funny. And I wasn't used to being laughed at. In Japan, women always treated men with great respect. Angry, I raised myself to a sitting position.

"Help me up," I demanded.

"Hush," she said. She pushed me gently back to the ground. "You were hurt. You need to heal before you move. Here, chew on this." She handed me a dirty root.

"It's filthy," I said.

"It will ease the pain," she said, and she brushed the root against her robe to clean it.

"I can't stay here," I told her. She was a stranger. I didn't want to tell her about my problems with Lord Oyama. He probably had more men searching for me. I said only, "I must go."

The woman laughed again. "Are all

samurai so busy?" she teased. "I don't think you're going anywhere. At least not until you're stronger." She offered me the root again. "Chew on it."

I did as she urged. I was too sick to argue. And she was right. The root did ease the pain. It sent a soothing warmth through me that took away the fire of the cut. She gave me cool water from a smooth clay cup. And then I slept again.

During the night, I woke only once. The cave was pitch black. The girl was gone. And outside I heard the sound of foxes barking.

In the morning she was back. This time she was dressed in pale gold silk, the color of winter grasses covered with frost.

"Perhaps you will be able to walk today," she said. She fed me a very odd broth. It looked disgusting. It was dark green and cloudy. It tasted even worse. As if it had been brewed from moldy leaves.

"What is this?" I asked.

"It will help you get well," she answered. "It will make you stronger."

The broth did make me stronger. By afternoon, I felt better. I could move my arm and put weight on it. I sat up and then slowly stood.

The girl watched with amusement as I reached for my sword.

"So now you are off?" she asked.

"Yes," I told her.

"It is not a good time," she said.

"What do you mean?"

She tilted her head to the side. "I hear hoofbeats," she said. "Six horses. They carry hunters. If you wait here, they'll pass."

I listened. But I heard only the wind in

the trees. The woman was imagining things. I moved toward the entrance of the cave, wanting to be on my way.

"Wait!" she said.

Maybe she wants something for her trouble, I thought. I reached into my pouch and took out a coin.

Anger flashed in her golden eyes. "You are a fool!" she snapped. "I told you the truth, but you don't believe me. I saved your life! And now you're going to throw it away!"

She *had* saved my life. And I was treating her like a serving girl. "Forgive me," I said. "I didn't mean to be rude. You've been very kind. And I don't even know your name."

"It's Mariko," she said softly.

"I am Shiro. Tell me, Mariko," I said. "Why have you spent the last five days in a cave, trying to save a samurai's life?"

She lowered her eyes and did not answer at first. Finally, she said, "I live in a village not too far from here. I found you bleeding and unconscious. I couldn't leave you to die." She looked at me curiously. "Don't you hear the riders?"

I listened again, and this time I heard a soft sound in the distance. Gradually it came closer, and I could make out that it was hoofbeats.

"How did you hear them when they were so far away?" I asked her.

Mariko shrugged and gave me a half smile. "I suppose I have sharp ears."

"Sharper than any man's," I agreed.

"So you will wait?" she asked.

I nodded and set down my sword.

Her amber eyes gazed at me, as if she could see through my skin. "You are hiding," she said.

"Yes," I admitted.

"Where will you go?"

"I don't know," I said. "Far from the lord who hunts me."

The sound of the horses grew louder, and we stopped talking. I crouched at the edge of the cave and watched the hooves pound by. Six horses, as she'd said. The riders all wore Lord Oyama's crest.

"I, too, have been hunted," Mariko said when the riders were gone.

"When?"

"A long time ago," she answered. "It was in another place, in another village. My family had enemies. We were hunted like wolves."

"What about the village where you live now?" I asked.

"It is hard to find and very small," she answered. "A few dozen houses on the side of a mountain. No one bothers anyone else. My neighbors leave me alone."

"What would they think of a ronin?" I asked. "I am an outcast now. A wanderer."

She studied me awhile before answering. "They would not trust you." She bit back a laugh. "They think all samurai are rich and spoiled. But they would not harm you either."

I thought of the riders searching for me. "How do I know the people in your village wouldn't sell me to Lord Oyama's men?"

"They wouldn't," she answered. "Not if you were with me."

"Are you so beloved?"

"The villagers and I get along," she said simply. "You're not fully healed yet. Come and let me care for you. You can leave when you're stronger."

I followed Mariko through the forest to her village. The girl moved lightly and surely, following a net of twisting paths that could only be found by one who knew them well.

Several hours later we came to a clearing. The village was just as she'd said. About thirty thatched-roof houses stood against the side of the mountain. Below them were rice and wheat fields.

"This is where I live," she said, leading me to the finest house of all. It was small, like the others. But instead of traditional bamboo-mat doorways, Mariko's house had sliding paper screens.

An old woman slid open the door and bowed.

"This is Hono," Mariko said. "She has served me faithfully since I was a child."

Hono nodded to me, then peered into

a pot that hung over the hearth. She lifted a wooden water bucket.

"Do you need water?" I asked her. "Let me fetch it for you."

Mariko frowned. "You're not that strong yet."

"I'm strong enough to carry water," I said. In fact, I was feeling much better.

Hono gave me the bucket. I went down to the well, which was in the center of the village. A group of barefoot children were playing there under the watchful eye of an elderly woman. The children scattered as I approached.

"Are they afraid of me?" I asked the woman.

"Not of you, samurai," she replied. "They're scared of the one who brought you here."

"Mariko?" I asked. "That cannot be.

Why would children be afraid of her?"

"She scares animals, too," the old woman said. "Look carefully. There's something strange about that pretty girl."

The woman was jealous of Mariko's beauty, I decided. After all, she was so old and wrinkled, you could barely find her eyes in her face.

I lowered the bucket into the well. "Mariko saved my life," I said. "I won't listen to wicked gossip about her."

The old woman nodded, as if she expected me to say that. "My name is O-Miwa," she told me. "Do you know what that means?"

"O-Miwa means 'the far-seeing,'" I answered.

"You are correct," she said. "What I see now is a blind young man."

I drew up the full bucket of water and

turned to leave. But the old woman's laughter stopped me.

"Your life is in great danger, samurai," she said. "And not from the men who are looking for you."

"Then from what?" I demanded.

O-Miwa cackled again. "From a beautiful woman who is not what she seems."

Chapter 3

The Mysterious Guest

I didn't take O-Miwa's warning seriously.
Why should I be afraid of Mariko?

I stayed with her and Hono for two
weeks. Each day, Hono brewed the odd
green broth, and Mariko tended my
wound. Though I tired easily, I could feel
my strength returning. By the end of the
first week I was able to chop firewood. At
the end of the second I could practice
swordplay.

Mariko saw that I was well again. "Are you leaving now?" she asked.

I didn't answer. I didn't want to go, and I didn't know how to tell her that.

I had fallen in love with Mariko! She was the loveliest woman I'd ever seen. And the cleverest. She could spin and weave cloth, paint and sing, and make delicate paper lanterns. And wherever she was, the smell of jasmine filled the air.

I had become used to the quiet murmur of her voice and Hono's as they worked in the garden. I liked seeing Mariko's things around me—the smooth wooden bowls we ate from, the pale green vase filled with flowers, her soft coral robe.

Lord Oyama's castle seemed like a lifetime ago. I didn't want to run anymore. In the tiny mountain village I felt as if I'd found home.

Mariko laughed at me again. "I ask you if you're going to leave and you stare at the sky. Is the question so difficult, samurai?"

I turned to face her. "No," I said. "I don't want to leave."

A smile played at the corners of her mouth. "Then stay."

"I want to marry you," I blurted out.

I didn't know what to expect. Would she say yes? No? Mariko suddenly became silent.

"You don't want to marry me?" I asked.

"A samurai can't marry a simple village girl," she said.

"You are far from simple," I told her.

"You haven't even known me a month," Mariko said. "You don't know what you're asking."

"I'm asking you to be my wife."

She looked at me, as if trying to see through to my heart. "Are you very sure?" she asked softly.

"I want to spend the rest of my life with you," I answered.

At last she smiled. "Then I will be your wife."

And so Mariko and I were married. Our wedding, like our meeting, was strange. In a land where there's a proper way to do everything, we broke many of the rules.

To begin with, I could not ask Mariko's family for permission to marry her. She had no family to ask. And I could not give her the traditional gifts that a man gives a woman before they wed. I had nothing to give except my gold coins, and Mariko wouldn't take those.

"Gifts don't matter," she told me.

"I'll make it up to you," I promised. "One day you'll have all the fine things you want."

"*You* are all I want," she said.

She gave me a wedding gift, though—a rich red silk robe. The back was embroidered with a gold dragon. The dragon's eye was a small, perfect emerald.

"Where did you find this?" I asked. "Surely such a fine robe wasn't made in this village."

"The robe was once my father's," Mariko answered. She never explained what had happened to her family. Talking about them seemed to upset her, and so I never asked.

We invited the people in the village to

the wedding. I asked O-Miwa, the head of the village, and the blacksmith. But they declined.

"Don't let it worry you," Mariko said. "I'll invite the others. You'll see, they'll come."

On the day of the wedding Hono cooked a feast of red fish and fried bean curd with rice. Mariko didn't have a traditional wedding dress. Instead she wore a robe of soft lavender with a silver sash. Pearls were strung through her night-black hair. She was more beautiful than the finest lady at Lord Oyama's court.

And once again Mariko was right. Almost everyone in the village showed up for the feast. But they ate little and drank even less. They came dressed in white—the color of mourning in Japan.

This is my fault, I thought. The villagers don't want to see Mariko marry a ronin. And who could blame them? I had no family, no lord, and no wealth. According to Japanese custom, a bride moves into her husband's house. I didn't even have a house to offer my bride. I moved into *her* home.

But Mariko seemed happy—until a man wearing a short blue jacket and dirty blue trousers entered the house.

He poured himself some rice wine. "To the bride!" he said, lifting his cup.

Mariko's face went pale with fear.

"What is it?" I asked her.

"Get him out of here," she said in a tight voice. "I don't want him in my house."

"Who is he?" I asked.

"I don't know," she said. Her voice was shaking.

"Mariko," I said, "I can't be so rude to

a stranger. He wants to wish us well."

"He wants to harm me, Shiro," she said. "Don't ask me why. Just make him leave now. Please!"

"Forgive me," I said to the man in blue. "But I must ask you to leave."

The stranger's eyes sought Mariko's. "Your bride doesn't want me here, does she?"

"No," I admitted.

"Then I'll go," the stranger said. "But please tell your beautiful lady that I'll see her again."

I turned back to Mariko and saw that she was even paler than she'd been before. The man was gone, but now O-Miwa stood in the open doorway.

Like the others, O-Miwa was dressed in white. She was holding a bunch of the scarlet lilies that grew at the edge of the rice fields. "Here are some special flowers for the bride," she said and laughed.

Mariko stared at the lilies and backed away. "No," she said, her voice pleading.

"I thought you liked flowers," O-Miwa said in a mocking voice.

"Get out!" Mariko shrieked.

"What is going on?" I demanded.

"It's the scarlet flowers," Hono whispered. "Bringing them into a house is bad luck."

"Why?" I asked.

Her answer gave me the chills.

"The person who brings them wishes that the house will burn to the ground."

The wedding ended badly. I ordered O-Miwa out of the house and sent the others home.

Mariko sat quietly. The color was drained from her face.

"What is wrong?" I asked her. "Who was that man? And why does O-Miwa dislike you? I do not understand."

"O-Miwa is just a spiteful old woman," Mariko answered.

"She's jealous of Mariko's youth and beauty," Hono said loyally.

"And the man?" I asked. "Have you seen him before?"

"No," Mariko said. "He doesn't live in the village."

"Then why did he frighten you?"

Mariko stood and touched my face. "I can't tell you," she answered.

It was the first of many things my wife could not tell me.

Chapter 4

The Red Silk Robe

What does a samurai without a lord do? Many ronin hire themselves out as soldiers. But I was tired of fighting. I needed something else to do. Something I was good at. I decided to train horses.

Our tiny village had only a few horses. All of them were slow, heavy plow animals. I needed lighter, quicker horses—those fast enough and smart enough to carry a man safely through battle.

I told Mariko about my plan. She was sitting on the porch, painting a paper lantern.

"There aren't any horses like that here," she said. "But there's a larger village, Nigoro. It's three day's walk from here. You'll find the horses you want there."

And so I set off for Nigoro. It took me four days to reach it, because I was still weak. But the journey went smoothly.

As Mariko had said, Nigoro was the place to buy good horses. There were several streets of shops and many large houses. I soon found a stable where I purchased a mare and her young colt. The owner asked a fair price. At the end of the deal, I still had some gold left. I decided to buy Mariko a belated wedding present.

In a crowded shop on a narrow street I

found a large, round mirror. I knew Mariko didn't have a mirror. This was the perfect gift. At last she'd know just how lovely she was.

As the storekeeper wrapped the mirror for me, I heard two women talking in the shop.

"Only the robe was stolen?" the first one asked.

The second one nodded. "Nothing else in the house was touched. It happened two weeks ago. My lord's red silk robe just disappeared. The one with the gold dragon on the back and the emerald eye."

The other woman clucked her tongue. "Who would do such a thing?" she asked. "Everyone in Nigoro recognizes Lord Yamada's robe. He was married in it!"

"It was such a mysterious theft," said Lord Yamada's servant. "That robe was locked in a chest. Only Lord Yamada has the key. He carries it with him all the time."

I listened in disbelief. The robe they described sounded exactly like the one Mariko gave me as a wedding gift. She'd given it to me almost two weeks earlier, just after Lord Yamada's robe disappeared. But how was that possible? Mariko had not left our village!

The first woman picked up a packet of writing paper and handed it to the shopkeeper. "I'll tell you how that robe disappeared," she said. "A fox stole it!"

A fox? In Japan people believe that foxes are creatures of mischief and magic. They're master thieves who can make themselves invisible. A fox can pass through locked doors, take what it wants, and leave everything else untouched. It can outwit the most careful man. Foxes have the gift of illusion. When you are under the power of the fox, you see what the fox wants you to see. Even things that don't exist.

And foxes have another power. They can change shape. A fox can take the form of another creature. Even the shape of a beautiful young woman.

It was possible for a fox in the form of a woman to enter Lord Yamada's room, open his locked chest, and steal the red silk robe.

But how did that robe find its way to my wife? That was a question I dared not answer.

Chapter 5

Bad Brings Worse

Mariko met me at the door.

"I see your journey was successful," she said, eyeing the two horses.

I looked at her. I couldn't ask if she'd stolen the robe she gave me. The thought was too absurd. Instead I said, "I brought back something else. Your wedding gift."

I handed her the wrapped mirror.

"Shiro, this isn't necessary," she protested.

"Open it," I said.

Looking flustered, she opened the package. She barely glanced at the mirror before covering it again.

"Mariko, look into it," I said. "I want you to see how beautiful you are."

"What foolishness," she said gently. "I don't have time to gaze at my own reflection. What we must do now is find a place for you to stable your horses."

"I'm going to build a stable," I said.

"But until you do, we'll need another place." She paused, then said, "I know. Old man Akira has that big barn. His horse died last year. The barn is empty now. Perhaps he'll let you keep your horses there."

"I will ask him," I said.

"I'll come with you," she offered.

We left the horses tied to a tree in

front of the house. Together we walked to old man Akira's land. We found Akira sitting outside his house, mending a basket.

"What do you want?" he called out.

"Only to ask you a question," I said. "I bought two horses, but I don't have a place to keep them. Would you let me use your barn until I can build a stable? I'll pay you for it."

The old farmer shook his head. "Bad brings worse," he muttered. "No, you cannot use the barn. Go somewhere else."

"You are very rude, old man," Mariko said in a quiet voice. "Are you sure you want to be so disrespectful to my husband?"

"Get out!" the old man shouted. "You have no right to bother me!"

"Leave him," I told Mariko. "I don't

want to go where I'm not welcome."

All the way home Mariko apologized for Akira's behavior. "I am sorry, my husband," she kept saying. "I never thought he'd be so rude."

"It doesn't matter," I told her. "It will just make me build the stable more quickly."

But the work took longer than I expected. I started by clearing the land behind our house. I cut down pine trees. Then I planed the wood into boards. Everything I did tired me. I couldn't understand it. My arm had healed, and yet I felt weaker. I could barely do a half day's work without resting. And even when I worked in the sun, I felt chilled. Ever since I went to Nigoro, I'd been unable to keep warm.

Three days after I began work on the

stable, Mariko came out of the house. Her eyes were shining. "I have good news," she called.

I put the ax down. "What is it?"

"You don't have to work so hard," she said. "You can keep the horses in Akira's barn, after all."

"Are you sure?" I asked. "What made him change his mind?"

"He did not change his mind," Mariko answered. "His wife has said it is all right."

"And Akira will listen to his wife?"

"He can hardly argue," my wife answered. "Old man Akira is dead."

Chapter 6

Akira's Widow

"Mariko," I said, "you should not look so pleased at another's misfortune."

Mariko's golden eyes held no emotion. "I am not pleased at his death," she said. "He's been sick for a while now. I'm only happy because now you have a place for the horses."

"The horses can survive outdoors."

"An icy rain will fall tonight," Mariko

warned. "I hate storms. Especially thunder. It frightens me. And the colt will have a hard time of it if he stays outside."

I looked around me. The sky was bright blue. The air was dry and warm. But Mariko was always right about the weather. She sensed things well before most people did.

"Very well," I said. "I'll talk to Akira's wife."

Akira's wife was a plain-looking middle-aged woman. Like most farmers' wives, her face was worn from a lifetime of hard work. She bowed to us and said we were free to use the barn.

By the end of the afternoon, Mariko, Hono, and I had cleaned out the stalls and settled the horses in their new home.

Mariko was delighted, but I was troubled. I'd noticed something odd. Every time Mariko went near the horses they shied. The colt even cried out in alarm. What O-Miwa said was true. The animals were terrified of her.

I was the last one to leave the barn that evening. Mariko and Hono had gone back home to prepare dinner. The cold rain that Mariko warned me of was already falling.

Akira's wife came out of her house as I slid the barn door closed. "Would you like some tea, samurai?" she asked.

"Thank you," I said. I wanted to go home. But it would have been impolite to refuse her offer.

The widow's house was dark and much smaller than Mariko's. There was only one drafty room with a fire pit in the middle.

I sat down, and Akira's wife gave me a

cup of green tea. She wore an old stained robe of thin cotton, but her hair was pulled back into a neat bun. There was something about her I trusted—a kind of courage that reminded me of the warriors I grew up with.

"I was sorry to hear of your husband's death," I said.

"Were you?" she asked. "Your wife didn't seem sorry."

"Akira was very rude to her," I said. "I don't think they got along."

She nodded and stared at the coals burning in the hearth. "My husband was a foolish man," she said. "Most people would not dare be rude to your wife."

"Are they afraid of me?" I asked. "Because I'm a samurai?" I touched the sword that never left my side.

"The villagers are not frightened by

you," the widow told me. "It is Mariko they fear. She is—" The widow hesitated, then said, "Not like the other women."

"She is not wrinkled and bent from working in the fields," I agreed. "Mariko is both beautiful and clever. Is that so terrible?"

A bitter smile flickered across the widow's face. "Perhaps she is too clever," she said softly. "Didn't you wonder why we wore mourning colors to your wedding?"

I felt my face flush red with shame. "I know that I am not a proper husband for such a fine lady. I—"

"Listen to me," the woman broke in. "*You* were the one we were mourning for. You are going to die. And soon."

Her words made no sense, and yet I believed her. "What are you—a fortune-teller?"

"I'm no fortune-teller," Akira's wife answered. "But I have seen Mariko's kind before. Your wife is different. She's not a woman. She's not even human. Don't you know what you've done, samurai? You've married a fox!"

Chapter 7

Trapped!

My sword was at the widow's throat before she could draw her next breath. "Take back your words," I ordered. "Then you can beg my forgiveness. No one insults my wife that way."

Akira's widow didn't even flinch.

"Kill me if you like," she said. "It won't change your wife. And it won't save you."

"Apologize!" I demanded.

"All you have to do is look at Mariko's eyes," the widow said. "They're the color of a fox's eyes."

"How can you blame her for that?" I asked. "No one chooses the color of their eyes."

"Do you know what a fox-wife does to her husband?" the widow went on. "She drains the life energy from his body. Slowly, he becomes weaker and weaker until he dies."

I didn't want to hear it. I pressed my blade against her throat until I broke the skin and drew a fine line of blood. "Apologize."

Still, I did not scare the woman. "Think, samurai," she said. "Are you as strong as you were before you met Mariko? If you are, then I have insulted your wife and deserve your anger. But if you recognize the truth in my words, then know you are living in a house of magic. And that magic will kill you."

I put the sword away and left the widow's house without another word.

Could Mariko really be a fox? My mind ran wild with questions. The "cave" where I first met her—was it really a fox's den? How come she could sense things long before anyone else? Why were animals and children so frightened of her? Why didn't she have friends in the village? Where did she get Lord Yamada's wedding robe?

And yet she was my wife, the woman I loved. I could not imagine Mariko hurting me—or anyone else.

Twilight was falling when I reached home. People from the village were on the porch and crowded around the house.

"Come out, fox!" they shouted. "Come out and we'll do to you what you did to Akira!"

Again I drew my sword. "Leave, all of you!" I ordered. "My wife didn't hurt anyone!"

Several of the men turned angrily. They were carrying rakes and pitchforks. It was late and I was tired. I barely had enough strength to stand. The last thing I wanted was a fight with my neighbors. "Please," I said. "Go home now. We can talk in the morning."

"There's nothing to talk about," the head of the village said. "Mariko killed Akira."

"Are you mad?" I asked.

O-Miwa stepped to the front of the

crowd. "No, samurai," she said. "You are blind. Three days ago you asked to use Akira's barn. He said no because he didn't want the fox-woman on his land. Now he is dead. And you have what you wanted. Surely, even you can see the connection."

"Nonsense," I said. "My asking to use the barn had nothing to do with Akira's death."

The others started shouting and moving toward me. They were going to attack. Quickly, I judged the odds. I was a trained warrior, the only one in the village with a sword. I would kill at least four of them. But they outnumbered me and I was weak with exhaustion. I would not win this fight. It was almost funny. All my life I'd prepared for a samurai's death. I always thought I would die on a battlefield fighting for Lord Oyama. Instead I was about to be torn apart in a tiny village by a bunch of angry farmers.

"Stop it, all of you!" said a woman.

Akira's widow pushed her way through the crowd. Even O-Miwa made way for her.

"You are all so brave!" the widow mocked the crowd. "An entire village against one man!"

"It's only right," the head of the village said. "The samurai's fox-wife took your husband's life."

The widow eyed him sharply. "My husband was sick for the last two years. You all know that. How can you be sure that it wasn't the disease that killed him?"

"Are you so sure it was?" the head man demanded.

"No," she said. "I don't know why my

husband died. But I won't let you use him as an excuse for more deaths. Do as the samurai says. Go back to your homes now."

The villagers obeyed her. Soon only the widow and I remained.

"I'm in your debt," I said. "I would not have won that fight."

"No," she agreed. "But you're still in danger. I don't think Mariko killed my husband, but she *is* killing you. A fox-wife takes a man's life energy and adds it to her own. Every day Mariko will get stronger. And every day you'll be closer to death." The widow's eyes were filled with pity. "You still don't believe me, do you?"

"How can I believe that my wife is evil?" I said numbly. "That she's not a woman, but a fox." I shook my head. "How can I believe that? I love her."

The widow looked at me and nodded. "May the gods help you."

Inside the house Mariko ran into my arms. "They wanted to kill me," she sobbed.

"It's all right," I told her. "I won't let anyone hurt you."

I meant to question her. Just for my own peace of mind. But weariness overtook me. Minutes after I entered the house I fell into a deep sleep.

The next morning I woke to the sound of Mariko's singing. She was probably outside, working in the garden. I turned over and my eyes widened. The pillow beside me was covered with fine white fur.

Chapter 8

The Hunter's Prey

Where had the white fur come from? I realized I did not want to ask Mariko. I couldn't bear it if my wife admitted that what the villagers said was true.

I dressed quickly and went outside. I didn't even know where I was going. Only that I needed to be far from the house. I walked up to Akira's barn, fed the horses, and then groomed and saddled the mare.

O-Miwa called out to me as I rode through the center of the village. "Only one man can help you now."

I reined in the horse. "And who is that?" I asked.

"He was the uninvited guest at your wedding," the old woman answered.

"The man in blue?"

She nodded. "His name is Kai. He lives in the forest. He's the one you need to find."

"And how do I find him?"

"There are trails," she said mysteriously.

"You never give me a direct answer," I told her. "I don't have patience for your games. Either tell me what I need to know or stop wasting my time."

The old woman stood and gave me a mocking bow. "A thousand pardons, samurai," she cackled. "How dare a poor peasant woman displease a great lord like yourself? Why, you could cut me in two with that sword of yours…"

Disgusted, I rode off. I was at the edge of the village when I saw Akira's widow working in the rice fields. She, at least, was honest.

"Excuse me," I said to her, "but do you know where I can find Kai?"

Surprise flickered across her face. In an instant, it was gone. "So you *do* believe me," she said. She pointed north and told me how to find the man named Kai.

I rode along narrow forest trails until the sun was directly overhead. I was near the top of a mountain when the trail forked to the left. Ahead I saw a small wooden house, with an even smaller hut behind it.

I hadn't even tied up the mare before Kai came out of his house. He wore the same dirty blue jacket and trousers he'd worn to the wedding. He was barefoot and unshaven. I could see that though he was a small man, he was strong. His arms were thick with muscles.

"Greetings, samurai!" he called cheerfully. "Did you bring your lovely wife with you?"

"I've come because of my wife," I said. "O-Miwa said you might be able to help me."

Kai nodded and sat down on the step that led into his house. "So, you've discovered what we knew all along. How does it feel to be married to a fox?"

I didn't answer his question, but said, "How long have you known Mariko?"

"I don't really know her at all," Kai answered. "The first time I saw her in human form was at your wedding."

"What do you mean?" I asked slowly.

"I mean, I have seen her as a fox," he said. He picked up a piece of bamboo from the ground, and took a small knife from his sash. He began to whittle the bamboo into an arrow shaft.

"She's a rare fox," he went on. "White as moonlight and swifter than running water. When she rubs her tail, she gives off fox fire as bright as any torch. She can even light your way through the rain."

I thought of the torches I saw the night I was attacked. They were neither the lights of travelers nor of a house. They were fox fire. That night when I'd nearly died I'd been found by foxes. And at least one of those foxes had been with me ever since.

"Tell me," I said to Kai. "How do you know that this white fox and Mariko are one and the same?"

Kai smiled. "That is my *business,* samurai."

"And why," I asked, "is Mariko so frightened of you?"

"Same answer," he replied. He dropped the arrow shaft to the ground and stood up and stretched. "Shall I show you what I do? Come with me."

He led the way to the small hut behind his house.

"I'm a hunter, samurai," Kai said. "And I can promise that your wife will never cause trouble again. Let me show you how I deal with foxes."

He threw open the wooden door of the hut. Four pairs of amber eyes gleamed dully in the light. Stretched across each of the four walls was the pelt of a dead fox.

Chapter 9

The Face in the Mirror

The hunter grinned and kept talking.

"First I set the snare. I bait it with fresh-killed chicken. Then I find the fox den. I smoke them out with burning pine needles and send them running toward the snare. When they're caught, I send an arrow straight to the heart." He snapped his fingers. "They're dead just like that. Quick and painless."

I walked away from the hut and sat down heavily. I felt ill. It was still hard for me to believe that Mariko was really a fox. It was impossible to agree to have her hunted and killed.

Kai squatted down in front of me. "I've never caught a white fox before. So I'll give you a good price," he said. He held out his hand. "One piece of gold, and I'll cure your fox problem. Your pretty wife will trouble you no more."

I stood up. "No thanks," I said. "*I* will take care of my own problems."

Kai's eyes traveled the length of my body. "You've lost weight since your wedding, samurai. You're thinner and weaker. It's hard to believe that you're a warrior to be feared."

"Believe what you want," I said. "But see that you do not harm the white fox."

"She's killing you," the hunter said. "Do you value your life so little?"

I got back on my horse and thought about his question. "I value my life," I answered. "But my life isn't worth much if I order the death of my own wife."

By the time I got back to the village, it was late in the day. As usual, I was worn out. And the sick feeling I'd gotten when I saw the dead foxes did not go away.

I took the mare back to the barn to feed and stable her. I slid open the barn door. The colt, who was tied up at the far end, was frantic. The little horse was rearing up, shrieking as if it were being beaten.

"What is wrong?" I asked, going over to calm it. I looked around the barn. There were only piles of hay and a few farm tools. What happened?

I held the colt's head and stroked it. "Your mother's back now," I said in a soothing voice. "There's nothing to be scared of."

But the little horse kept tossing its head. Finally, I realized that something above us was scaring it. I gazed up. Was an owl in the rafters?

Near the roof of Akira's barn were paper-screen windows that could be slid open in the summer. Outlined against the closest window was an unmistakable shadow. A long snout, two pointed ears, a slim, light body, and a thick bushy tail—the shadow of a fox!

I raced out of the barn. But the fox was gone. How could it have gotten up that high? I asked myself. Was I imagining things? Was the colt?

Shaken, I went back into the barn. The colt now quietly nuzzled its mother. I gazed up at the window. There was no shadow, no sign of a fox. Had it really been there?

They say that a man who has a fox-wife slowly starts to lose his mind. He forgets things. He cannot tell black from white or north from south. He is always in confusion.

I knew I was losing my strength. As I groomed the horses, I wondered if I was also losing my mind.

Everything that had gone wrong was my fault. From the moment I fled Lord Oyama's castle, I broke *wa*. Wa means harmony. It also means that people should act the way they're supposed to. A samurai should serve his lord. A man should court his bride properly. If you break the rules, you go outside the harmony. And once you do that, there is no protection.

As a boy, I was taught not to be afraid. But now I was terrified. I knew I had to go home and face Mariko. If she was truly a creature of evil, it was my duty to put an end to her. And yet I couldn't bear to think of life without her. I would have to take her life and my own as well. I didn't leave the barn that night until well after darkness fell.

Mariko was not in the house. I found her sitting in the garden. There was a full moon. Her back was to me. Her black hair shone in the moonlight against her pale golden robe. She was bent over something on the ground. Staring at it as if she could do nothing else.

I walked up behind her, not wanting to disturb her, not wanting to begin the awful questions I had to ask.

And then I realized what she was doing. She was gazing into the mirror I gave her.

"Mariko," I said softly.

She didn't move.

I stepped closer to her. I saw her reflection in the mirror. It was the face of a white fox! The fox's face was framed by my wife's black hair and her pale golden robe—but the creature before me wasn't my wife.

The fox-woman suddenly turned with a cry. The golden robe fell to the ground, and Mariko's long black hair vanished. My wife was gone.

I was standing in the moonlight, facing a white fox with amber eyes. The animal gazed at me for a long time, as if trying to tell me something. Then she gave a long, mournful howl and vanished into the night.

Chapter 10

The Fox's Spell

I didn't stop to think. I tore off after the fox. She was as swift and cunning as Kai had said. She ran from our garden to the rice fields. From the rice fields into the pine trees that border the village. And from the pines up into the mountains.

The spry fox didn't bother with trails. She scrambled up slippery hillsides. She darted through the thickest brush. She leaped from the top of one boulder to the next. Again and again I had to slow down and cut through brush or pull myself up rocks. Several times I was sure I'd lost her. And then I'd see a glimpse of silver-white fur in the distance, and the chase would begin again.

I hadn't gone far before I felt weary. I was breathing hard. My legs and chest ached. I was shivering with cold. But I couldn't let the white fox get away.

And so I followed, not caring where she led me. I followed her for hours—until the moon had moved through the sky. At last she stood on the rim of a ravine, her white fur glistening as if it were made of moonlight.

She saw me, too. I'm sure of it. Her topaz eyes gazed at me, and she cried out.

The forest darkened as a cloud slid in

front of the moon. I stumbled toward the ravine. But when I reached the top, the fox was gone. And I was lost.

I looked around. I had no idea of where I was. Below I heard the sound of water running. It could have been any of the hundreds of streams and creeks in the mountains.

I walked the mountain all night long. My body ached, and I longed for sleep. But I wouldn't let myself rest. I was afraid that if I didn't find the white fox, I'd never see Mariko again.

Finally, I had to give in. My feet could go no farther. My legs refused to hold me up. I swayed, dizzy. Then I sank to the forest floor, unable to move. Finally, I slept.

I dreamed of the hunter. Kai was standing

in front of his hut, circled by foxes. There were red, gray, brown, and even black foxes. But there was no white fox.

A huge red fox sat directly in front of Kai. Animal and hunter stared into each other's eyes. The fox lifted his left paw. Kai lifted his left hand. The fox tilted its head to the side. Kai did the same. Whatever the fox did, Kai copied like a wooden puppet. The meaning of the dream was clear. The hunter had fallen under the power of the foxes.

I awoke to someone turning me over onto my back. Cool fingers pressed against the side of my throat.

"Well, you still have a heartbeat," said a man's voice. His laid a palm across my forehead. "And a fever. Can you hear me?"

I opened my eyes. Dawn was turning the night sky pearl gray. A monk knelt beside me. "Can you remember your name?" he asked.

"My name is Shiro," I said, sitting up. My body ached all over, but I did not seem to be badly hurt.

"Did you fall?" he asked. He was an older man with a shaved head and a kind face.

"No," I answered. "I was chasing a fox. I chased her until I was too tired to go on."

The monk frowned. "Surely you could catch the animal in a snare. Why would a young samurai spend the night chasing after a fox?"

"Because I married her."

"Ah." The monk rocked back on his heels. He studied the sky for a moment.

"A man with a fox-wife. It is indeed a problem.

"Are you trying to kill her?" he asked abruptly.

"I don't know," I admitted. "I think she's killing me. But I don't want to harm her. She once saved my life. I'm in her debt."

The monk nodded. "Is she a good wife? When she is not a fox, I mean."

"I love her," I said simply. I felt like a fool. A man so blinded by love that he loved the evil that was taking his life.

The monk squinted. "When your wife is a fox, what color is she?"

"White," I said. "Does it matter?"

"White foxes are often connected to the rice god, Inari," the monk explained. "We may be able to ask Inari for help. There's a chance we can save your wife—

if she's willing to let go of the fox."

"What do you mean?" I asked.

"She would have to come with us to the Inari shrine and pray for help."

"I don't know if I'll ever see Mariko again," I said. "But if I do, I'll ask her."

The monk sighed. "Don't be too hopeful. A fox-wife is an unusual creature. She has the keen senses of an animal, the beauty of a woman, and all the magic of a sorceress. She may not want to give up that kind of power. And the transformation is dangerous. If it works, she will be your own dear wife. If it doesn't, it will kill her."

Chapter 11

Another Death

The monk helped me to my feet. I stared in amazement. I was in a small stand of trees, just beyond the village rice fields. I was no more than twenty yards from the village!

"What's wrong?" the monk asked, seeing my confusion.

"How did I get here?" I asked. "I fell asleep in the mountains. I was miles away from the village."

"Were you?" the monk asked softly.

"I walked for hours last night!"

"That does not mean you walked for miles," the monk said with a chuckle. "Don't you know that when you're under the power of a fox, you're in confusion. You see what the fox wants you to see. You feel what the fox wants you to feel, and go where she wants you to go.

"I would guess that last night—no matter where you *think* you traveled—you never once left this grove of trees."

The priest told me where I could find the Inari shrine, then bid me good-bye.

Two more surprises greeted me that day. As I walked through the village, I saw O-Miwa sitting at her place beside the well.

"You have no hope now, samurai," she called out.

"Are you talking in riddles again?" I replied.

"The hunter is dead," she told me.

"What?"

"The head of the village found him this morning," O-Miwa reported. "He was kneeling in front of his hut. Something chewed on him. Bit him till he bled to death." She nodded at me, as if we shared a secret. "The foxes got him."

I thought of my dream, and I knew she was right. But I said nothing. I shrugged and walked back to my own home.

Or what used to be my home. The house I'd shared with Mariko was no longer the same. It was a ruin, a house deserted long ago. The roof was falling in. The porch was covered with old boards and barrels. Inside, the straw mats and the fresh flowers were gone. Dust covered the floor. The walls smelled of decay.

"Mariko?" I called. "Hono? Is anyone here?"

There was no answer, of course. It was plain to see: No one had lived in the house for years.

I went out into the garden. Yesterday, jasmine and wisteria had grown here. Now there were only weeds. I rubbed my eyes. Was this a dream too? Had I imagined Mariko's house? Or had it all been an illusion created by a fox? I *was* losing my mind. I could no longer tell what was real and what was not.

I don't know how many hours I sat in the weed-filled garden. I was numb. Mariko was gone. The house was gone. I wasn't even sure they'd ever existed.

Sometime during the evening I heard

footsteps in the garden. Akira's widow walked toward me. She held a steaming bowl in her hands.

"You must eat, samurai," she said. "You have little enough strength as it is."

"What do I need strength for?" I asked. "Everything that mattered to me is gone."

"Eat anyway," she said.

Akira's widow saw to it that I drank all of the broth. Then she returned to her house. I stared at the ruined garden until my eyelids began to close. But as I lay down to sleep I saw something gleaming in the grass. It was Mariko's mirror!

Perhaps, I thought, it *wasn't* all a dream. I fell asleep with the mirror in my hands.

When I woke, the moon was overhead,

bathing the village in brightness.

I sat up, chilled and aching. Shivering, I wrapped my arms around myself. And then my heart began to pound so hard I thought it might leap from my chest.

The white fox sat at the base of a willow tree. Her tawny eyes were watching me.

"Mariko?" I asked, afraid to allow myself to hope.

The fox nuzzled something at her feet. I saw it was a white bone—the jaw bone of a horse. She picked it up in her mouth. And then slowly the fox began to change.

Her body stretched into the slim, graceful body of a woman. The white fur on her body became smooth and loose and golden, until it turned into a robe of golden silk. The fur around her head grew longer and darker until it was no longer white fur but long midnight-black hair. Then a fine mist covered the long muzzle and pointed ears. When the mist cleared, Mariko's beautiful face appeared. I saw that one thing remained the same in fox and woman. Akira's widow was right. Mariko had a fox's eyes.

I bit down on my lip to make sure I was awake. "Is—is it really you?" I stammered.

"I've missed you, my husband," Mariko answered.

"Why are you here?" I asked. "Did you come back to stay with me?"

"No," she said quietly. "If I stay with you, you'll die. And I love you too much for that."

"I'll die just as quickly if you leave," I told her. "I don't want to live without you."

Mariko covered her face with the long sleeve of her robe. I knew that she was crying. I wanted to comfort her. But first there were answers I had to have.

"Is Hono a fox as well?" I asked.

Mariko dropped her sleeve and wiped her tears away. "Yes," she answered. "Hono is a gray fox. She's one of the oldest foxes and is very wise."

"Did you kill Kai, the hunter?" I asked.

"My kin did. He killed too many of us. They couldn't let him go on."

"And old man Akira?"

"Akira died of the disease that was eating at him for the last two years." Mariko's golden eyes held mine. "You are the only one I've hurt—and the only one I care for. I don't know what to do, Shiro. But I had to see you one last time."

I had one more question. "Where did the red robe you gave me come from?"

Mariko dropped her eyes. "From Nigoro," she answered in a quiet voice. "I stole it from Lord Yamada. He never wore it." She looked at me again. "I wanted to give you something wonderful."

"None of that excuses stealing," I told her.

"Excuses it?" Mariko was laughing again. "A fox doesn't need an excuse to steal. Theft is as much a part of my nature as breathing." Her laughter stopped. She took the mirror from the ground and stood beside me. "Look," she said.

Together we gazed at the reflection—a black-haired woman with a fox's face. "Your mirror doesn't lie," Mariko said. "This is what I am, Shiro. This is why I must leave you."

"Not if you'll give up the fox," I said and told her the monk's suggestion.

Mariko was quiet for a long time after I finished. "I don't know," she said at last. "I have always been a fox. I can't imagine what it would be like if I couldn't see what a fox sees or hear what a fox hears."

"You'd be a woman like any other," I told her.

"And would you still love me if I were so ordinary?"

"I love you even as a fox who's taking my life," I told her. "That can never change. But if you give up the fox, then you and I can be together."

Mariko nodded, but I could see tears at the corners of her eyes. "All will be well, my husband," she said. "If I survive the change," she added, almost to herself.

The tawny eyes suddenly blazed with

fire. "At midnight on the dark of the moon, I will meet you at the Inari shrine," she promised.

Then the woman was gone. The white fox stood in her place. Startled, I blinked. When I looked again, she was gone.

Chapter 12

The Hour of Magic

The half month from full moon to the dark of the moon passed slowly. I stayed in the village. I worked with the horses and helped Akira's widow with her farm. In exchange she let me sleep in the barn. The work kept me busy, but all I could think of was Mariko. What would happen on the night of the dark of the moon? Would my wife return to me? Or would I lose her forever?

I watched the moon each night. And each night I looked for the white fox. But

I never saw her. It was as if she'd never existed. At last the moon waned to a thin sliver of light. On the next night the skies would be black.

I sent word to the monk that Mariko had agreed to our plan. He would meet us at the Inari shrine. The monk sent a drawing—a map. I didn't worry about Mariko finding the shrine. A fox could find anything. But would she change her mind? I couldn't blame her if she decided not to risk her own death.

The next morning I set off on the mare. I studied the monk's map. The shrine was high in the mountains. It would be a full day's ride. But I was feeling stronger now that I no longer lived with a fox.

I followed the web of trails all day long. Higher and higher we climbed. As the afternoon wore on, dark clouds gathered over the mountains. At dusk a cool wind began to sweep through the trees. The mare began to get skittish. A storm was blowing in.

The rain began as darkness fell. The trail hugged the side of the mountain. The mare moved slowly, carefully placing each foot. I knew better than to rush her. One wrong step and we'd tumble down the sheer rock slope. The wind grew so strong, it felt as if it was trying to sweep us over the side.

There was no moon. The rain hid the stars. It was the darkest night I'd ever known. It was possible I'd ride right past the shrine and never even see it.

Still, we followed the trail. I was soaked and shaking with cold. I began to wonder if I'd somehow taken a wrong turn. Or if I was once again caught in the fox's confusion. Perhaps this journey, too, was illusion. For all I knew, the mare and I were riding endless loops around a village rice field.

At last I saw two torches burning in the distance. Fox fire, I thought. But as I drew closer I saw that they *were* torches. Torches that lit the base of a long flight of stone stairs.

I tied the horse loosely to a tree. I wanted her to be able to get away if I didn't return. I started up the stairs.

Like many shrines, this one had several flights of stairs with hundreds of steps. Each flight was steeper than the one before. And the stones were slick with the rain.

I reached the top of the first flight. There were no torches here. Candles burned inside two stone lanterns. By their light I saw narrow white pieces of wood sticking out of the ground. I shivered harder. I realized I was surrounded by graves!

I'd never worried much about ghosts or spirits. But now I wondered. What would happen when I finally reached the shrine? I would be alone in a storm with a monk, a fox, and the spirits of the dead.

I saw two glimmers of light above me. I kept climbing the staircase. I passed an old, abandoned teahouse. There was still so much farther to go.

The rain let up a little as I finally reached the top. Here two more torches burned. Their flames blew wildly in the wind. The monk was waiting beside a tall red gateway.

He bowed to me and took one of the torches. I took the other and followed him through the gate into a courtyard. The building must have once been a grand temple. I could see gold leaf on the broken roof.

Holding the torch before me, I peered inside. If there had been statues or scrolls, they were long gone.

"This temple is abandoned," I said to the monk. "Why did we come here?"

"For the foxes," he replied. "I will show you."

He led me through the empty temple building to an overgrown courtyard behind it. Two white stone foxes sat in the long grass. Each statue was as tall as a man.

"These foxes are the messengers of Inari, the rice god," the monk explained.

"If you are troubled by fox magic, it's wise to pray to Inari's foxes."

"Can they change Mariko from fox to woman?" I asked.

"If you are lucky," the monk replied. He peered at me more closely. "Where is your wife?"

"She said she'd be here at midnight," I replied.

The monk nodded. "Magic is strongest at midnight."

The monk began to prepare the shrine. He burned incense and placed lit candles around the fox statues. Then he started a low chant.

I sat and waited. In the distance I heard the crash of thunder.

"That's not a good sign," I said. "Mariko's afraid of thunder."

"Yes, that makes sense," the monk

said. "The thunder god and foxes have never gotten along."

"What if she doesn't come?" I asked.

The monk looked at me with sympathy. "Then you have lost a wife."

At midnight, something shifted. It felt as if the very air had changed. And the elements as well. Fire, metal, wood, water, and earth were all different. The fire in the torches now burned bright green. When I reached for my sword, my hand passed through the blade. The trees in the courtyard grew taller until even the temple roof was dwarfed. The rain that came down stung like hail. And the earth beneath our feet seemed to hum.

It was the hour of magic. And something unearthly had entered the temple courtyard.

Chapter 13

Crescent Moon

I stared at the two white fox statues. They looked like ghosts in the darkness. Then a third white fox sat between them. This fox was alive and gazed at me with familiar amber eyes.

"Your wife?" the monk asked.

I nodded.

The monk bowed to the fox. "If you are willing," he said, "I will start the ritual. If Inari's foxes grant my prayers, you won't be a fox anymore. You'll simply be a woman. Do you understand?"

There was the sound of laughter, and suddenly Mariko stood in front of us. She wore a silvery-white robe, the color of her fox fur.

"Of course, I understand," she said to the monk. "Do you think I would be here if I did not?"

"If you wanted to trick your husband, you might," the monk said.

Mariko's amber eyes flashed with fury. "Don't insult me, monk," she said.

"I beg your pardon," the monk said. "I will begin the ceremony. Both of you must kneel before the foxes. Ask them to help Mariko. Ask them to help her let the fox go."

We did as the monk said. We prayed for hours, as the rain came down. The monk chanted and waved white strips of paper over Mariko. The thick smoke from the incense burned our eyes. Thunder crashed and lightning split the sky. The ground trembled, and the statues began to sway.

Mariko fell to the ground. I went to her side. She was breathing, but I couldn't wake her. A fox's shadow slowly rose from her chest. It hovered above her for a second. Then it raced away between the two stone foxes.

"Mariko?" I said.

But Mariko did not answer.

I turned to the monk, more frightened than I'd ever been. "What just happened?" I asked him.

"I don't know," he replied. "We must wait and see."

We stayed at the temple for two days. I held Mariko in my arms. She never opened her eyes or made a sound. Only the rise and fall of her chest showed me that she was still breathing.

The monk stayed with us. He brought me rice cakes and water. He told me not to give up hope. But I knew he thought Mariko was dying.

"She couldn't survive the transformation, could she?" I finally asked.

He shrugged. "Perhaps she was too much fox to ever be fully human."

"Now she's not even a fox," I said sadly. "She's only a woman who will never wake up again."

"You have so little faith, samurai," murmured a light, playful voice.

I cried out as Mariko rubbed her eyes. Slowly she sat up and gazed around the courtyard.

"I am very hungry," she said. "Do you have anything to eat?"

Then she turned to face me. I stared at her as if she were a ghost. Mariko's eyes were no longer amber, but a rich, dark brown.

She touched my face with her hand. "What's wrong, my husband?" she asked gently.

"Your—your eyes," I stammered. "They're no longer like a fox's."

"Oh, I know," she said with a laugh. "I can't see nearly as far now. Or hear as well. And the earth doesn't smell quite as sweet."

"Then you're sorry you changed?" I asked. I waited, dreading her answer.

"Sorry?" she said. "At night I will miss being able to see so well," she admitted. "But what I have given up, I give gladly. Now you and I can truly be together, Shiro. You won't get weaker every day.

No more stealing. No more illusion."

Slowly she stood up and bowed to the monk. Then she bowed deeply to Inari's two white foxes.

We set off together under the light of the crescent moon.

Ellen Steiber is the author of the Bullseye Chiller *Fangs of Evil*. She lives in the desert in Tucson, Arizona, and has always loved stories about animals and magic. Some of her favorite stories are about Kitsune, a mystical Japanese fox. Although there aren't many foxes in Tucson, Ms. Steiber often sees coyotes scampering past her office window. She's pretty sure they're magical, too.